Upsy Daisy

www.dk.com

LONDON • NEW YORK • STUTTGART • SYDNEY

www.dk.com

Editor   Vicci Parr
Designers   Mandy Sherliker and Ness Wood
Managing Editor   Joanna Devereux
Managing Art Editor   Chris Fraser
Production   Linda Dare
DTP Designer   Jill Bunyan
Original TV Script   Jocelyn Stevenson
Story Adaptation   Caryn Jenner
Photography   Dave King
Illustrations   Denis Ryan

First published in Great Britain in 1999 by
Dorling Kindersley Limited, 9 Henrietta Street, London WC2E 8PS

A CIP record for this book is available from the British Library.

ISBN 0-7513-6640-4

Colour reproduction by Dot Gradations Limited
Printed in Belgium by Proost

It was time for Mopatop to open his shop.
"Welcome to Mopatop's Shop," he said.
"Would you like a cosy little bed? Or lots of
pretty red? Or a bunny on his head?"

DING!
The shop bell rang and
in walked a possum
with a toolbox.
"I'm Upsy Daisy," said
the possum.
"Of course! I forgot you
were coming today,"
said Mopatop.
"I'll get to work right
away," said Upsy Daisy.

"Hello, Mopatop!" Puppyduck called. "What's going on?"
"Upsy Daisy is fixing up something special for us."

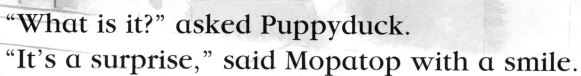

"What is it?" asked Puppyduck.

"It's a surprise," said Mopatop with a smile.

"All done," said Upsy Daisy. "Payment will be one poem, please."

Mopatop cleared his throat:

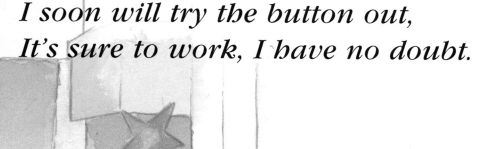

Thank you, thank you, Upsy Daisy,
It's plain to see you are not lazy.
I soon will try the button out,
It's sure to work, I have no doubt.

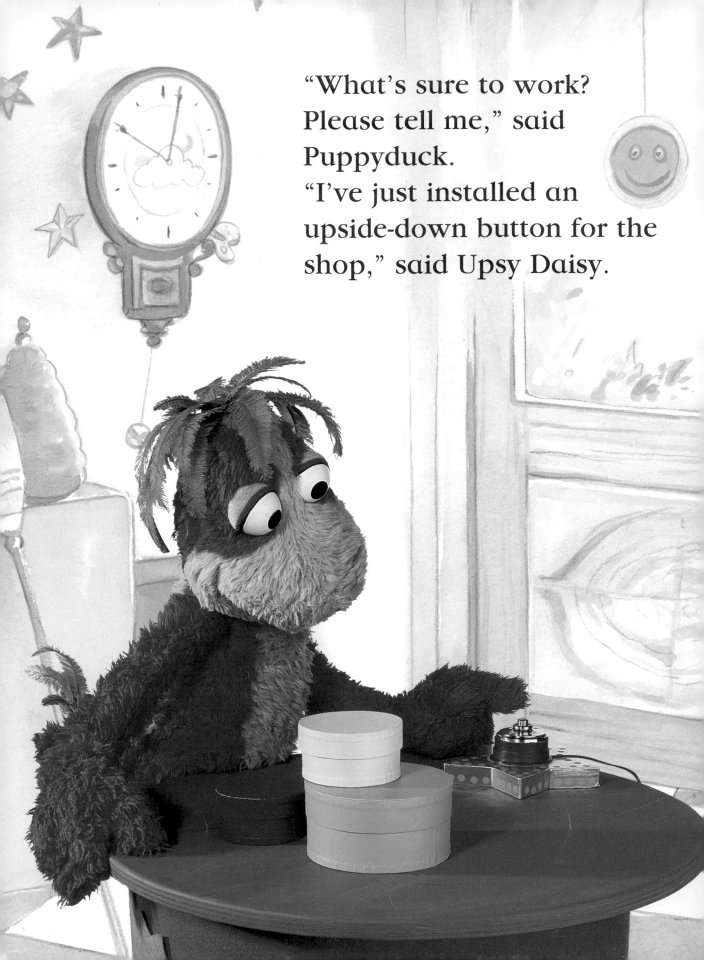

"What's sure to work? Please tell me," said Puppyduck.
"I've just installed an upside-down button for the shop," said Upsy Daisy.

"You mean that if
I press this button,
I'll be upside down?"
asked Puppyduck.
"You certainly will,"
said Mopatop.

"The whole shop
will be upside
down," said Upsy
Daisy. "Call me
if you have any
problems. Bye!"
Puppyduck pressed
the button.

Suddenly, the shop turned upside down.
Puppyduck didn't like being upside down.
"I feel weird," she said. "The floor is now
the ceiling."

"Mopatop, please turn the shop right-side up again," cried Puppyduck.
"All right," said Mopatop, and he pressed the button.

The shop turned right-side up.
DING!
"Here comes a customer," said Mopatop.
The customer was a big furry animal.
"Hello, I'm a gnu. I saw your shop turn
upside down and I was wondering if I could
try some upside down, too!"
Mopatop pressed the button.

The shop turned upside down again.
Moosey was in the attic.
"Oh no, not again!" he groaned.
"What's wrong, dear?" asked Mother Mouse.
"Don't you like being upside down?"

"I rather like being upside down," said
Father Mouse.
"I don't," said Moosey with his head in his
hands. "I like being right-side up."

"This is excellent," said
the gnu. "How do we get
right-side up again?"
"Like this," said Mopatop,
pressing the button.
Nothing happened.
Mopatop frowned. "The button
is stuck. We'll have to call
Upsy Daisy."
All together they called, "UPSY DAISY!"

DING!
As soon as Upsy Daisy walked through the
door of the shop, she turned upside down.
"You called?" she said.
"Yes," said Mopatop. "The button is stuck."
"Can you fix it, please?" asked Puppyduck.

"Of course I can fix it," said Upsy Daisy.
"But I'll need an upside-down song first."
"I can't sing upside down!" said Puppyduck.

Mopatop and the
gnu sang:
The world's turned upside down,
The bottom's now the top.

I much prefer the way it was,
The time has come to STOP!
finished Puppyduck.

"That was a beautiful song. Thank you," said Upsy Daisy. "Now I will fix your upside-down button."
Upsy Daisy got out her tools and went straight to work.

Suddenly, the shop turned right-side up.
"Hooray!" cheered Puppyduck.

But a moment later, everything was upside down again. The attic was upside down, too. "Oh no," groaned Moosey. "I want to be right-side up."

Suddenly, he *was* right-side up.
"At last, somebody's listening to me," said
Moosey. "I don't feel very well at all."
"This is rather fun," said Father Mouse.

In the shop, the gnu turned to leave.
"Thank you very much for showing me
upside down," he said.
"My pleasure," said Mopatop. "Goodbye!"
Upsy Daisy put her tools away.
"I've got some bad news, Mopatop.
Your upside-down button
is broken."

"I don't think we need an upside-down button after all," Mopatop told Upsy Daisy.

"But what about the poem and the song you gave me?" she asked.

"Will you be wanting them back now?"
"Poems and songs are for sharing," said Mopatop.
"Oh, thank you!"
And Upsy Daisy sang all the way out of the shop.

Just then, the big clock chimed.
"That means it's time to close the shop," said
Mopatop. "Puppyduck, where are you?"

Mopatop looked all over
the shop.
"I'm over here!" said a
voice from behind the
little door.

Mopatop opened
the little door.
"Bunny and I
were practising
upside down," said
Puppyduck.
Mopatop laughed.